D1594889

Jacques et la Canne à Sucre

Jacques et la Canne à Sucre

A CAJUN JACK AND THE BEANSTALK

By Sheila Hébert-Collins
Illustrated by Alison Davis Lyne

PELICAN PUBLISHING COMPANY
Gretna 2004

*To the students and staff of Manatee Elementary
in Naples, Florida, who respect and welcome
cultures from around the world*

*The word "Pelican" and the depiction of a pelican are trademarks
of Pelican Publishing Company, Inc., and are registered
in the U.S. Patent and Trademark Office.*

Library of Congress Cataloging-in-Publication Data

Collins, Sheila Hébert.
    Jacques et la canne à sucre : a Cajun Jack and the beanstalk / written by Sheila Hébert-Collins ; illustrated by Alison Davis Lyne.
        p. cm.
    Summary: A Cajun version of Jack and the Beanstalk that features magic sugar cane cuttings, a gigantic plantation home, and a fiddle that plays Cajun music. Includes pronunciations and translations of Cajun words and a recipe for Shrimp or Crawfish Etouffé.
    ISBN 1-58980-191-1 (hardcover : alk. paper)
    [1. Fairy tales. 2. Folklore--England.] I. Lyne, Alison Davis, ill. II. Jack and the beanstalk. English. III. Title.

    PZ8.C.C6953Cj 2004
    398.2--dc22

                                            2003027706

French editing by Barbara Hébert Hébert

Printed in Singapore

Published by Pelican Publishing Company, Inc.
1000 Burmaster Street, Gretna, Louisiana 70053

Jacques et la Canne à Sucre

Once upon a time deep in the Louisiana bayou country, there lived a poor widow, *Jacqueline Boudreaux,* and her son, *Jacques.* Jacqueline and Jacques lived in a houseboat right there on Vermilion Bayou. Near the bayou was a huge crawfish pond where Jacqueline and Jacques could catch crawfish to sell in Lafayette.

Jacqueline Boudreaux (zhah-KLEEN BOO-dro)—a Cajun name
Jacques (zhahk)—French for Jack

They were very poor because they only made money during crawfish season. Every week Jacqueline would send Jacques to town to sell a sack of crawfish. They would use part of the money to make groceries and the rest they would save in a coffee can they hid under a bed.

On the last day of crawfish season, Jacqueline called out, *"'T Jacques, viens voir ici!* Dis here is my prize sack of crawfish. I've been fattening dem up all season. Dey will bring a nice price. If we get fifty dollars for dat, it will last us till next crawfish season. *Dépêche-toi,* before doz other crawfish farmers get to de market!"

'T (tee)—short for "petit," a nickname
viens voir ici (vee-yehn vwahr ee-SEE)—come see here
dépêche-toi (day-pesh-twah)—hurry up

Jacques put the sack of crawfish in his wagon and left for town. When he got to Maurice, he was halfway there, so he decided to take a rest. As he rested next to a big oak tree, an old Cajun in a wagon passed by, then stopped.

The old Cajun got out of the wagon
and walked over to Jacques.

"'*T garçon,* what you got in dat sack, dere?" asked the old Cajun.

Jacques answered proudly, "Dat's my momma's prize crawfish. Dey so fat dey gonna bring us fifty dollars dere in Lafayette."

"*Mais, non, 't garçon,*" said the old Cajun. "Dat's not gonna bring more dan twenty dollars. I tell you what. How 'bout I give you five dollars and dese magic sugarcane cuttings?"

't garçon (tee gahr-SOHN)—little boy
mais (meh)—well
non (nohn)—no

"Now, dese cuttings are filled with *gris-gris* and will produce a field of sugarcane in three days. Just think what money dat will bring you, *cher*. And your momma will be proud of you, yeah."

Jacques scratched his head and then said, "I think dat's a good deal. You right. My momma sho will be proud." He traded the crawfish for the money and the cuttings, then took off for home.

gris-gris (gree-gree)—magic
cher (sheh)—my dear fellow

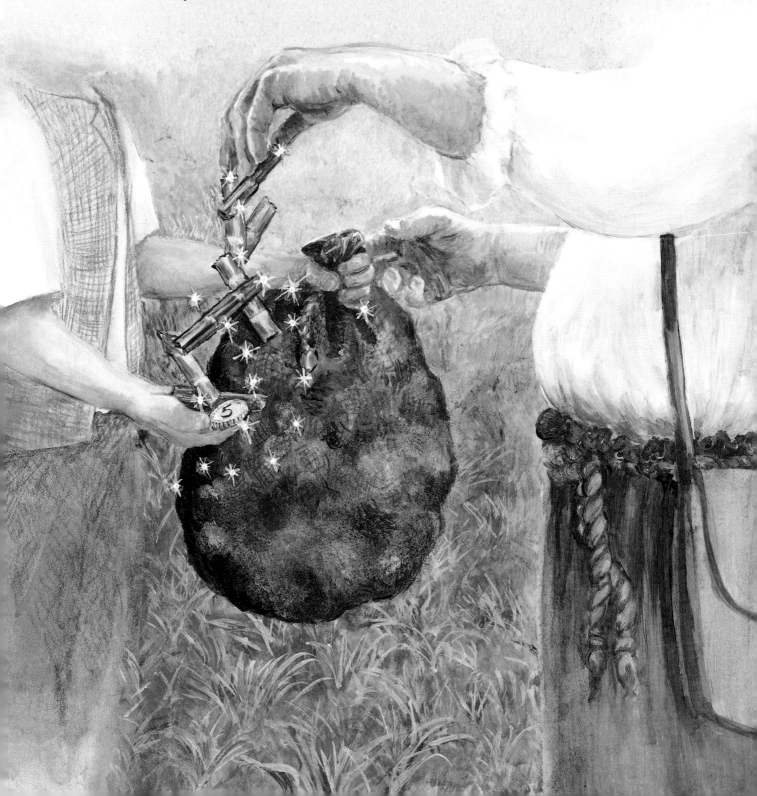

When Jacques got back to the houseboat, Jacqueline was waiting for him. "How much you got for dat crawfish, *mon fils?*" she asked. With a proud smile, Jacques replied, "Look, momma. I made me a good deal, yeah. I got me five dollars and dese magic sugarcane cuttings dat will make us rich sugarcane farmers!"

"You *cooyon!*" Jacqueline screamed. "We will surely starve dis winter!"

mon fils (mohn feess)—my son
cooyon (koo-yohn)—crazy

She grabbed the cuttings, threw them into the bayou, and then snatched the money. "Go to bed, 'cause dere's no gumbo for you tonight!"

Jacques sadly walked to his room and went to bed. The next morning his growling stomach woke him. He looked at the window, surprised that it was dark. Up against his window were big leaves. What could this be? He jumped out of bed and went outside. There right beside the houseboat grew an enormous sugarcane stalk. It reached above the clouds.

"Momma, Momma, *viens voir!*" he shouted. Then he started climbing the giant stalk. Jacqueline came outside and saw what Jacques was doing. "*Arrête ça.* Come down! *Vite!*" she yelled. But Jacques never looked back. He just kept climbing through the clouds, higher and higher.

arrête ça (ah-RET sah)—stop that
vite (veet)—quickly

Jacques climbed all day. He thought, *Ça finit pas!* But finally the sugar-cane stalk did end, and Jacques stepped off into a beautiful field of rice.

In the distance, he could see a big plantation home. He trudged through the rice field until he came to the mansion, ten times larger than any he had seen along the bayou.

ça finit pas (sah fee-nee pah)—it won't end

There on the veranda was a huge rocking chair with a fiddle leaning against it. Jacques walked over to the huge doors and looked through the keyhole. He saw a long hall but no one around, so he quietly turned the big doorknob and tiptoed in.

Jacques walked down the hall, which led to a large kitchen.

There on the kitchen table were plates of *bonne cuisine*.

bonne cuisine (bun qwee-ZEEN)—good food

Jacques was so hungry! He climbed up a large chair and, standing on the chair, helped himself to the feast. There was more than he could ever finish. As he ate, he looked around the table and spotted a small chest filled with bags of gold.

All of a sudden, Jacques heard thundering footsteps coming down the hall and then a voice that roared, "Fee, fi, fo, fum! I smell the blood of a Cajun man. Be he alive or be he dead, I'll grind his bones for my bread."

Jacques grabbed a bag of gold, jumped to the floor, and hid behind a large sack of rice. Into the kitchen walked a giant of a man, at least ten feet tall.

Jacques knew the giant must be an Englishman to hate Cajuns like that. The giant sat down in his chair and said, "I must have been smelling that good Cajun food too long because there's no Cajun here. Good thing, too," he added. When he had eaten all the *étouffée,* jambalaya, gumbo, and French bread, he yelled out, "Woman, bring my magic fiddle and *poulet!*"

étouffée (ay-too-FAY)—stew
poulet (poo-LAY)—chicken

In walked a Cajun *maw maw* carrying a fiddle and a chicken with feathers of gold.

maw maw—old woman

She put them on the table, then started clearing off the dishes. The giant roared, "Lay, *poulet*, lay!" To Jacques's surprise, the chicken laid a golden egg.

Then the giant commanded, "Play, fiddle, play." In amazement, Jacques heard that fiddle play *"Allons danser, Colinda."* As it played, the giant started to fall asleep. This was Jacques's chance. He wanted to bring his momma that *poulet* and fiddle so she'd never call him *cooyon* again.

"Allons danser, Colinda" (ah-lohn dahn-say, co-lin-dah)—
"Come Dance, Colinda," a popular Cajun song

So Jacques climbed up the chair, grabbed the *poulet* and the fiddle, and jumped to the floor. As he ran, the fiddle started playing *"J'ai passé devant ta porte,"* louder and louder, waking the giant. When the giant heard his fiddle, he turned and saw Jacques sprinting for *la porte.* He jumped from his chair and chased Jacques. Jacques ran straight for the sugarcane stalk as fast as he could, with the giant close behind.

"J'ai passé devant ta porte" (zhay pah-say duh-vahn tah port)—"I Passed by Your Door," a popular Cajun song
la porte (lah port)—the door

Jacques quickly slid down the sugarcane stalk. As he came close to the bottom, he yelled, "Momma, *vite, vite*—get de ax!"

When Jacques was safely on the houseboat, he and Momma
started chopping down that sugarcane stalk. Before long, it
was swaying. Finally it came crashing down, giant and all.

"*Pooh yi,* Jacques. What you got yourself into dis time?" asked Momma. "*Mais,* nothing but good fortune, Momma," Jacques proudly answered. Then he showed Momma the gold, the magic *poulet,* and the fiddle.

pooh yi (poo yie)—a Cajun expression meaning "oh, my"

From that day on, Jacques and Jacqueline had all the money they needed and good Cajun music to pass a good time. *C'est tout!*

c'est tout (say too)—that's all

SHRIMP OR CRAWFISH ETOUFFEE

8 oz. fresh mushrooms, sliced
1 large onion, chopped
1½ sticks butter
3 lb. peeled, deveined shrimp or 1-2 lb. packaged crawfish tails, preferably from Lafayette or Breaux Bridge
Salt and cayenne pepper to taste
1 can cream of mushroom soup
1 can cream of celery soup
1 pt. cream

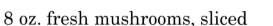

Sauté mushrooms and onions in butter until onions are clear and limp. Do not brown.

If using crawfish, do not wash off yellow fat. Season shrimp or crawfish with salt and cayenne. Add shrimp or crawfish to vegetables and simmer for 10 minutes.

Add soups and cream. Simmer for 20 minutes, stirring often.

Serve over rice. Add French bread and salad. *Ça c'est bon!*

ça c'est bon (sah say bohn)—that's good